CONTENTS

KARATE
REBELS

TEXT BY SALIMA ALIKHAN

ILLUSTRATED BY PULSAR STUDIO
(BEEHIVE)

raintree

Raintree is an imprint of Capstone Global Library Limited, a company
incorporated in England and Wales having its registered office at 264 Banbury
Road, Oxford, OX2 7DY – Registered company number: 6695582

www.raintree.co.uk
myorders@raintree.co.uk

Text © Capstone Global Library Limited 2021

Originated by Capstone Global Library Ltd
Printed and bound in the United Kingdom

978 1 3982 0428 7

British Library Cataloguing in Publication Data
A full catalogue record for this book is available from the British Library.

CHAPTER 1

SPARRING CHAMP

Aliyah circled her sparring opponent, Suma. The other karate students sat cross-legged around the sparring mat. Aliyah blocked out the familiar sights and sounds of the dojo.

She ignored the weight of her sparring gear. She focused on making her breath come from deep inside her belly.

Suma Samadi-Kroft was twelve, the same age as Aliyah. The brown belt around Suma's waist was tied tight.

Suma was quick and light on her feet. She easily danced out of the way of Aliyah's jabs and kicks. But Aliyah knew Suma's one weakness. Suma often forgot to block, leaving herself open to kicks and punches.

Adrenaline rushed through Aliyah's veins. Suma was good, but Aliyah still knew she'd win. She always did.

Aliyah had won every brown-belt sparring match since she'd arrived at the dojo two months ago. But there was nothing quite as satisfying as beating Suma. Nothing, that is, except being sure that she was going to get black belt first.

"Keep your guard up," Sensei Juarez reminded Suma. She turned to Aliyah. "Work on your kicks."

Aliyah studied Suma. She knew that Suma tended to drop her back hand.

Aliyah could go in for a back fist strike and then kick. Suma was so fast that Aliyah would need to reach to get to her. If she pushed Suma out of the ring, that would be a point in Aliyah's favour. But Aliyah really wanted to land a kick. A kick was worth two points.

Aliyah went for it. She got Suma to the edge of the ring with a series of back fist strikes. Then she started throwing out kicks at her weak side – a roundhouse, a side kick, just trying to land something.

Suma dodged them all. Finally Aliyah went for a middle roundhouse kick to Suma's floating ribs.

Suma staggered, dropped to her knees, and tapped out.

Sensei stepped in and held two fingers over Aliyah's head. "Two points!" she called.

Aliyah took a deep breath. She bowed to Suma and smiled to herself. Sensei always said the greatest power was patience, but Aliyah believed something different.

Aliyah knew the greatest power was winning.

Aliyah went to take off her sparring gear. She felt light and free with it off as she stretched. She knew she'd be a black belt in no time.

She'd been doing this for five years. She loved everything about the dojo – from the sound of feet on the mat to the equipment heaped around the edges of the room.

She rejoined the class just as they were kneeling around the mat in seiza. They bowed and recited the dojo kun, or "rules" of the dojo, like they did at the end of every lesson:

"First: Show good character. First: Be sincere. First: Show effort. First: Practise etiquette. First: Practise self-control."

In Aliyah's dojo, the dojo kun weren't numbered. They were all labelled the "first" because none of the kun were more important than the others.

The last one – self-control – always made Aliyah squirm a little. But she pushed the thought out of her mind. She told herself that those old karate masters must have known that sometimes you had to lose control if you wanted to survive.

Aliyah took off her belt and folded it carefully. She'd been a brown belt for what felt like a long time. She was readier than ever to step up to black belt.

CHAPTER 2

DOJO KUN

After the lesson, Aliyah and Suma headed to their kit bags. Suma's face was calm and her eyes were shining. Aliyah couldn't figure Suma out. Why was she in such a good mood, even after losing?

"Hey, Aliyah, some of us are going out for ice cream," Suma said. "Want to come?"

Aliyah stared at her. She didn't get why Suma was always trying to hang out with her. In Aliyah's experience, people didn't usually want to be her friend. "No thanks."

Suma rolled her eyes. "This is just a karate lesson, Aliyah. Just because we spar doesn't mean we're enemies. We're allowed to be friends."

Aliyah zipped up her kit bag and didn't respond. She couldn't imagine not taking karate seriously. Karate was the most important thing in the world.

"Hey, Aliyah." Sensei Juarez walked over to them. "Come here and chat for a minute."

"Are you in trouble?" Suma whispered.

Aliyah gave her the cold shoulder. Trying to ignore the dread building in her chest, she picked up her bag and followed Sensei to a corner of the dojo.

"I wanted to check in and see how you're doing," Sensei said. "I know things have been tough for you the last couple of months, and that you had a hard time at your old school. I just want to caution you against aggressiveness. You know that karate students must never be drawn into fights easily. If we misuse what we learn, we bring dishonour on ourselves."

Aliyah looked at the floor. Sensei had talked to Aliyah's parents, so her teacher knew all about her history. She always thought she did her best to hide what she was feeling from Sensei. But sometimes, it felt like Sensei could read Aliyah's mind.

"You've made a lot of progress since you got here," Sensei went on. "I believe in you. How are you adjusting to the dojo?"

"I like the dojo," Aliyah said.

"I know things can be different for you here, especially if you work hard and remember the dojo kun," Sensei said.

She put her hand on Aliyah's shoulder and continued.

"You're very talented, Aliyah, but karate is about more than winning. It's about taking care of each other. Remember, we are not here to hurt each other. We are here to help each other."

Aliyah shrugged. She couldn't help being annoyed, but she tried not to let that show on her face.

Sensei had no idea that sometimes, being good at a martial art was the only thing that saved you. The fact that Aliyah could take on most people in the class made her feel safe.

But she didn't say that to Sensei. She just nodded. "Okay. Thank you. I'll remember."

"All right, good," Sensei said. "See you next time."

Aliyah zipped up her jacket. She picked up her bag and left as fast as she could.

CHAPTER 3

MISSING HOME

Outside, Aliyah's dad was waiting for her in their old, worn out car. He didn't say much when she slid into the back seat. He just nodded and started the car.

"Can we hurry?" Aliyah looked anxiously out the window. She didn't want Suma, whose dads were picking her up in their fancy new car, to
see them.

"Was karate good today?" Aliyah's dad asked as he pulled away from the kerb.

"Yeah," Aliyah mumbled.

She slid down in the seat as Suma's parents' car passed them. Then she sat back up again and stared out the window. They drove home in silence.

She'd lived here for two months, but it still felt strange to her. Before they moved here, she'd lived all her life in a nearby town, Springfield. She couldn't help comparing the streets of her old neighbourhood with these streets. Nothing felt familiar.

Plus, back in Springfield, she'd lived with both her parents. But then they got divorced. She missed living with both of them, even if her parents fought all the time.

She glanced at her dad. A stab of guilt went through her. If it wasn't for all the problems she caused at her old school, they probably wouldn't even be in this new town.

"No fights today?" her dad asked.

Aliyah wanted to say, "You don't have to ask me that every single time you pick me up." Instead, she just took a deep breath and gritted her teeth. "No fights."

It made her so angry. First Sensei, now her dad. People seemed to think that all she could do was fight. Just because she got in fights in her old school. Many, many fights. But she had won them all.

"Aliyah, I know this has been hard for you," her dad said.

"I don't want to talk about it," Aliyah said softly.

She couldn't wait to get out of the car. As soon as they parked in front of their apartment building, she ran up the stairs, let herself in with her key, and went to her bedroom. She closed the door and turned on the music.

She flopped down on the bed and stared at the ceiling. The apartment was so quiet, unlike their old house.

She'd first heard her parents fighting a couple of years ago. Aliyah remembered them yelling at each other in the bedroom of their old house. She'd crouched outside their door, wishing the yelling would stop.

She remembered wondering why her parents were fighting. She thought maybe it was because of something she'd done.

She knew she wasn't the perfect kid, like some other kids seemed to be. She had a hard time listening in lessons sometimes. A few times, the teacher had even had to call her parents.

Could that be why they were fighting? she'd wondered. Were they so annoyed at her that it was making them fight?

She'd felt so angry inside that the next day in school, when Suzie Miller said something snotty to her, Aliyah hit her. She'd never used her karate training to hurt another kid, but she did that day.

After that, Aliyah had got into so many fights at school that her parents made her stop taking karate. Soon after, her parents separated, and she moved to this new town with her dad.

After she begged him to let her take karate again, he let her join Sensei Juarez's dojo. But she knew if she ever got into fights at school again, her dad would make her stop taking karate for good.

Sensei had been very kind when Aliyah arrived at the dojo. Sensei said to remember the dojo kun when practising the kata.

She also told Aliyah that aggressiveness

was different from anger. She said the difference was that it was normal to feel anger, but that aggression was usually an act or attitude that hurt another person. She explained that karate fighters could learn to use their anger, without being aggressive.

She told Aliyah to pretend her anger was like a red-hot crystal ball inside her that got smaller with every exhale. When Aliyah tried it, it didn't really work, but she never told Sensei that.

Sensei didn't know Aliyah's biggest secret: Whenever Aliyah wondered if it was her fault that her parents split up, she still got so angry that she wanted to hit someone.

Aliyah glanced out of her window. It faced the car park. She thought of Suma, who was probably out somewhere eating ice cream with her friends.

She felt a little tug in the pit of her stomach. She thought of going to school in the morning, and the tug got bigger.

It wasn't easy being the new kid at school. She knew it would be useless to try to get to know her classmates. Once they got to know her, they'd realize what a troublemaker she was, and they wouldn't want to be friends with her anymore anyway.

She also knew if she caused problems with other kids, she'd lose karate. And she had promised herself she would never lose karate again.

She reminded herself that she'd be at the dojo after school again on Thursday. Her safe place. There, she was one of the champions. There, she could beat almost anyone.

She smiled to herself.

CHAPTER 4

NEW KID AT SCHOOL

On Thursday afternoon, Aliyah streamed into the dojo along with a group of other pupils. She bowed in, dropped her bag on the floor by the wall, and prepared for the lesson.

After bowing in seiza, the class stood and lined up according to belt colour. Sensei led the warm-ups: jogging in place, skipping, sit-ups, push-ups and stretches. Then she took them through their basic training drills, called kihon: blocks, strikes, kicks and stances.

When they had finished with kihon, Sensei announced, "We have a new pupil joining us today. Everybody please welcome Zoya, Suma's younger sister."

Aliyah looked at the frowning little girl standing next to Sensei. A yellow belt was wrapped around her waist. She had Suma's dark eyes and brown skin.

Instead of wearing Suma's smiley expression, though, the little girl scowled and stuck her tongue out at her sister.

Suma sighed and rolled her eyes.

"Let's break out and run through techniques," called Sensei. She hadn't seen Zoya stick out her tongue.

The class broke into groups according to belt colour. Aliyah walked around, helping students with their techniques, which the

brown belts were often asked to do.

She paused when she got to the yellow belts. Suma was already there, talking to Zoya. Zoya was scowling even more than before.

"I need you to behave," Suma was saying. "You need to be respectful if you want to stay in this dojo."

"You're not my boss," Zoya said. "Stop telling me what to do!"

"Fine!" Suma said. "Get kicked out again. I don't care." She turned and stomped away.

It was the first time Aliyah had ever seen Suma upset. The yellow belts started practising side kicks again. Aliyah noticed that Zoya had good concentration, balance and speed, but no technique.

Aliyah walked over to their group. "You

need to lift your leg more and slow down," she told Zoya.

Zoya stopped and glared at her. "Who are you?"

"My name's Aliyah. And if you ever want to get further than yellow belt, you'll have to learn to slow down." She shrugged and added. "I can show you. Or not. It's up to you."

Zoya studied Aliyah with narrowed eyes. Finally, she said, "Fine. Show me."

Aliyah pulled her aside. "Okay, we're going to go through this really slowly. Make sure your heel's higher than your toes, and that your front hand is up for balance. Bring your knee up, and now extend your leg."

She positioned Zoya's leg for her.

"Remember the higher you kick, the more you'll have to pivot," Aliyah said. She showed her an example kick. "And remember to turn your support foot. Here, try to line up your chest, your bottom and your heel."

She helped steady Zoya until the younger girl could balance a bit better. She watched her do a couple of side kicks, then walked away to help another group. But Aliyah kept glancing back at Zoya, who was still practising kicks. She was a little wild and unbalanced, but there was determination on her face.

Aliyah smiled to herself. If Zoya kept up that determination, she'd get past the messiness.

A second later, a commotion came from the yellow belts.

"Get off me!" someone cried.

It was Zoya. She'd launched herself straight at one of the other kids and knocked her to the ground.

CHAPTER 5

REMIND YOU OF ANYONE?

Sensei rushed across the dojo and pulled Zoya off of the other girl. "That is absolutely not how we conduct ourselves in this dojo, Zoya," Sensei said, helping the other student back to her feet. "Are you all right?"

The other girl nodded, but she looked shaken.

"I'd like you to apologize, Zoya," said Sensei.

Zoya crossed her arms. "I don't have to listen to you. You're not my parent."

CHAPTER 6

Taking a Chance

After class, Aliyah found Suma sitting near the gym bags. "Thanks so much for helping out today, Aliyah," Suma said. "I can't believe Zoya let you teach her something."

Aliyah shrugged, embarrassed. "That's okay. Don't worry about it."

"I don't know what we're going to do with her," Suma went on, sniffling. "She's getting in fights all the time. My parents thought it would be a good idea to send her to this dojo, but now I don't know."

Suma looked so miserable that Aliyah couldn't help feeling sorry for her.

"She's got to be allowed to stay in karate," Aliyah said, surprising herself. "It'll help her. It helped –" She almost said, *It helped me*, but stopped herself. "It helps lots of people."

Suma wiped her nose. "I really want her to stay in karate too. But at the same time, she can't keep acting like this if she expects any dojo to train her."

"Does she let you teach her anything at home?" Aliyah said.

Suma shook her head. "She started training two years ago, but she never gets beyond yellow belt because she won't apply herself."

Aliyah glanced across the room at Zoya. She bit her lip. She thought of how she'd been at Zoya's age – like a little tornado, wanting to attack everything in her path.

She remembered how much worse she'd got once her parents' fights got bad. She thought about how many teachers and her old sensei had tried to work with her. Her cheeks burned.

"What if maybe . . . what if I try to work with her?" Aliyah asked.

"Are you serious?" Suma jumped to her feet. "You know what, I think that could work! She seems to like you. It's worth a shot!"

Suma threw her arms around Aliyah. Startled, Aliyah stepped back. Suma was too happy to notice. "My parents will really appreciate it!" Suma said.

Aliyah flushed. She'd never heard of a parent appreciating anything she'd done. She hoped she knew what she was doing.

"I'll go ask Sensei," she said. And soon she had permission.

CHAPTER 7

A NEW PUPIL

Aliyah arrived early for their next karate class. Zoya was waiting for her inside the dojo, her arms crossed. "My sister asked you to work with me, didn't she?" she demanded.

Aliyah put her kit bag down against the wall. As she pulled out her gear, she remembered that when she was younger, she always wanted people to be honest with her.

"No. I volunteered," she told Zoya.

Zoya narrowed her eyes. "Why did you volunteer? Nobody wants to work with me."

"Well, I do."

Zoya looked surprised. "Are you going to boss me around? Because you're not one of my parents, either."

"I can't boss you around about the important stuff," Aliyah said. "*You* need to decide if you want to be part of this dojo. But if you stay, you'll have to follow the dojo rules. No more losing your temper and hitting people." She paused. "Even if you feel that they deserve it."

This time she saw a small smile tug at Zoya's mouth.

"We don't learn karate so we can hurt people," Aliyah said.

Zoya frowned and said, "Sometimes I can't help it."

"I know it feels like that," said Aliyah.

Her stomach twisted a little. "But we can learn to use our anger in a helpful way. Because it's not always possible to just pretend we're not feeling lots of stuff, right?"

Zoya nodded slowly. "Yeah, I can't do it."

Aliyah decided to confess to Zoya. "Can I tell you a secret? Sometimes, I get really angry and scared. About all kinds of stuff."

Zoya's eyes got huge. "Do you?"

"Yep. So here's a trick I learned. I imagine my feelings are a little red ball of light inside me. When I breathe, the ball gets smaller and more focused. I imagine that I can direct it through my legs or arms when I'm hitting a target, and I send all that energy into the target. That way, I don't have to try to pretend my feelings aren't there. And this helps me stop thinking about wanting to hurt someone. It just focuses my energy."

She turned red, thinking of all the times she'd wanted to beat Suma. That, plus the fact that the little red ball of light trick hadn't worked for her yet.

"Okay." Zoya sounded uncertain. "I don't know if I can do that. But I can try."

"It takes practice," said Aliyah. "What's your goal in karate?"

"I want to go to a tournament!" Zoya said right away.

"Then you have to learn techniques," said Aliyah. "And slow down."

Zoya balled up her fists. "Will you help me get good enough to go to the tournament?"

"You mean the regionals competition?" Aliyah said. "That's in three months."

Zoya nodded hard.

Aliyah took a deep breath. "We can try. I can't promise anything. Three months is not much time, and you have a lot to learn."

"I don't care," Zoya said. "I want to go and prove I'm good."

Aliyah understood that. "Okay. I can try to help."

"Can we start soon?" said Zoya, bouncing on her feet. Other pupils were starting to trickle in.

"Yeah. We can start after the lesson today, if your parents are okay with you staying a little later," said Aliyah.

"Okay!" Zoya replied.

Aliyah watched Zoya skip off to get in line as Sensei walked into the room. The knot in her stomach loosened a little bit.

Maybe, just maybe, this would work after all.

CHAPTER 8

LEARNING FROM TEACHING

After their next class, Aliyah stayed late to spar with Zoya.

"You're relying on speed alone," Aliyah said to her, once they'd started. "You're going to have to show some technique in here. Remember to block!"

Zoya glared from under her headgear as she bounced on her toes. She lifted her fists in blocking position.

"Come on, try for a kick," Aliyah said.

Zoya was reluctant. Aliyah knew Zoya avoided kicking because she thought Aliyah was too tall for her. Instead, Zoya threw wild punches and forgot to block, which left her open. Aliyah sent a side kick into Zoya's stomach. She didn't want to hold back. Zoya had very little time to prepare for the tournament.

"Check your technique and block!" Aliyah said.

She decided to try tiring Zoya out. When Zoya was tired, she wouldn't be able to count on her speed anymore. She'd be forced to start relying on technique.

Aliyah wondered if Zoya would keep showing enthusiasm once she realized how hard she was going to have to work. But Zoya kept going, even when she was so tired she was practically falling over.

"I'm going to go to the tournament!" she said.

"Just remember winning isn't everything," Aliyah said. "If that's all you think about, you won't be able to enjoy practising."

"How do you know?" said Zoya.

"Trust me, I know," said Aliyah. "There's lots more to karate."

"Yeah, like what?" Zoya demanded.

"It's about inner strength and respect, and about helping each other become better fighters," Aliyah said. Then she added, "Remember the dojo kun. And breathe deep. The more you train, the more you'll be able to channel your feelings into the kicks and strikes."

Suddenly Zoya stood very still. "Like my feelings about my grandma?" she asked.

"Yes." Aliyah nodded. Her belly flopped a little. "If you miss your grandma, it's okay to feel all that. If that makes you sad or angry, you can put those feelings into your fighting."

Zoya nodded. Aliyah was pleased to see that she took more time during that session to get things right.

Over the next few training sessions, Sensei Juarez would come watch them. "You need more discipline, Zoya," she said. "And you'll have to work on your balance with kicks."

Zoya sometimes glared at Sensei, but she managed not to talk back. She'd just turn around and start punching at Aliyah again.

Little by little, Zoya learned to slow down. She learned to stay light on her feet and to block at the same time.

After training one day, Sensei pulled Aliyah aside.

"I'm really proud of how you've been working with Zoya," she said. "Are you thinking of competing in regionals this time?"

Aliyah hesitated before answering. She'd thought about competing, of course. She already had plenty of awards from previous competitions. But this time, for some reason, her heart wasn't in it.

A strange thing had happened to her. The longer she worked with Zoya, the more she remembered her parents fighting. But instead of just feeling angry all the time, she often felt sad about it too.

Somehow, the sadness made it easier to picture the little red ball of light and focus while she struck and kicked at the punching bags and targets. She didn't have the same feelings of wanting to hurt someone.

"Not this time," she said, surprising

herself. "I want to focus on getting Zoya through regionals this time around."

Sensei smiled.

"I really like how you've been helping Zoya work with her emotions," said Sensei. "You've reminded her that it's okay to be angry. Sometimes we're cross for good reason."

Aliyah got that uncomfortable feeling again that Sensei could see right into her soul.

"The more we learn and practise," Sensei said, "the more we learn that karate is about taking all our feelings and learning how to use them."

"Do you think Zoya will learn how to use them?" Aliyah asked.

"With you teaching her, she's got a really good chance," Sensei Juarez answered.

After about two months of training Zoya, Aliyah arrived at the dojo to find the sign-up poster for regionals on the wall.

Zoya came racing towards her. "Aliyah! I've signed up! I'm ready! I know I am!"

Aliyah smiled. "That's great, Zoya."

Suma came over to join them. "This is so exciting! Well done, Zoya!" She turned to Aliyah, smiling. "And, by the way, want to spar? You're getting rusty."

Aliyah glared at first. Usually, Suma's suggestion that she was getting rusty would have made Aliyah feel red-hot with anger. But now she pictured the red ball of light. She still felt angry, but she no longer felt like she wanted to punch someone.

"Fine. Let's go and get ready," Aliyah said.

A few minutes later they were circling on the mat. Aliyah went for a strike almost right away, and Suma blocked without dancing too far out of the way. Suma was staying close today, striking more than kicking.

Aliyah was dying to land a jump spinning hook kick, but Suma would see it coming a mile away. Flashier moves could be easily anticipated. They weren't always as effective as sticking to simpler moves. In the end, Aliyah took Suma out with a foot sweep.

"That was close, Aliyah," Suma teased. She stood up, panting. "Good job."

Aliyah bowed to her. "Thanks," she said.

For the first time, she meant it.

CHAPTER 9

REGIONALS

"You should eat something, Aliyah," her dad said.

It was the morning of regionals. Aliyah tried to force herself to eat a banana. She was running through a mental checklist of all the things she'd taught Zoya. She hoped Zoya would remember at least some of them in such a high-pressure environment.

She put the rest of her banana down.

"Are you all right?" her dad asked.

"I am. I just hope Zoya will be," Aliyah replied.

The drive to the regionals seemed to take forever. As soon as they got to the gym, everything inside the huge space felt familiar. Aliyah felt a little pang of regret that she wasn't competing this year.

Suma, Zoya and their dads were near the front doors, checking Zoya in for the tournament.

"Hi!" Aliyah called, rushing over to them. "Are you ready, Zoya?"

Zoya gazed around the crowded gym with wide eyes. She tightened her belt. "Yeah."

One of Zoya's dads stretched out his hand to greet Aliyah's dad. "Hi, it's so nice to meet you. We've heard so much about Aliyah. We're so grateful she's working with Zoya. You must be very proud of her."

Aliyah's dad smiled at her. "I am. She's done a great job."

The praise made Aliyah's heart warm up, but she was still feeling too jittery about Zoya's match to think about much else. "Thanks, Dad. Come on, Zoya, let's go over to your area."

They headed over to the 6–10-year-old yellow belts section. Aliyah looked around at the other kids already waiting there. There were only two of them.

"Where is everybody?" Zoya asked Aliyah.

"Sometimes there are very few competitors in certain categories," Aliyah told her.

She noticed one of the other kids – a boy – was crying. His parents and a first aid person were with him.

"What happened?" Aliyah asked.

"He sprained his ankle practising, I think," a woman who seemed to be his mother said. "He's out of the match."

Zoya looked amazed. There was only one other girl waiting to spar.

"So it's just me and her?" Zoya whispered, pointing at the other girl.

"Looks like it," said Aliyah.

"I'm nervous," Zoya gulped.

Aliyah hugged her. "You're going to do great. Stay focused, and don't use up all your energy straight away. Just remember to block. And don't let your guard down."

"You're dead!" the other girl shouted gleefully. "I'm gonna pulverise you!"

Zoya's jaw dropped. Then she clenched her fists. "You wanna say that to me again?"

"Zoya, Zoya." Aliyah pulled her aside. "Don't worry. A lot of kids do that. They taunt each other and get each other worked up before they get in the ring."

Zoya scowled at the other girl. "Yeah, well. I don't like her."

"Your best bet is to draw it out." Aliyah coached. "The match is timed at five minutes. Get your opponent tired, work them all the way up to the end, and don't leave yourself open. Slow it all down. And remember the little red ball of light."

Zoya nodded slowly.

"I'll be right here watching," Aliyah added.

"Promise?"

"Promise. I won't go anywhere," Aliyah said, as Suma, her parents and Aliyah's dad came and joined them.

Zoya and the other girl were called to compete. Zoya went to join her opponent on the mat. She and the other girl bowed to the referee and then to each other. Zoya's face was red.

Aliyah remembered how furious she always got when her opponents teased her before competing. She tried as hard as she could to send Zoya a telepathic message: *Ignore it. Just ignore it.*

The match began. Aliyah saw straight away that Zoya's opponent had a plan. The girl was going to try to get Zoya to use up all her energy. Then she was going to really let Zoya have it.

Zoya's opponent landed a kick to her side. Zoya stumbled a little, but her face was more determined than ever.

Aliyah held her breath. She watched Zoya breathing deeply, gathering her energy. She started going for quick jabs while dancing out of the opponent's way. Aliyah could see the other girl getting more and more frustrated. She was trying to drive Zoya to the edge of the ring, but Zoya wasn't letting her.

Finally, the judge called, "Break. Time's up. Ten points red. Ten points white. Tie score!" They'd hit five minutes, with no clear winner.

Zoya looked confused. She remembered to bow to the referee and bow to her opponent. She touched the other girl's glove and said, "Good match."

Then she came flying over to Aliyah and her family.

"What does that mean?" she said.

"It means the judges have to decide how they're going to award points," said Aliyah. "Since you both tied and you were the only two contestants, it means they need to break the tie to give you both a place."

Aliyah jiggled her foot nervously, while Zoya, Suma, their dads and Aliyah's dad waited nearby. What would Zoya do if she didn't get first place?

Finally, the judge's voice rang through the air.

"In the 6–10-year-old yellow belt category," she called, "second place is awarded to Zoya Samadi-Kroft!"

Zoya stared. Aliyah held her breath. She was sure Zoya might be angry. But instead Zoya shouted, "Second place! Whoa! Not bad for my first tournament!"

CHAPTER 10

REAL WINNING

While Suma and Zoya's family all hugged and congratulated Zoya, Aliyah went over to her own dad. To her surprise, he reached out and hugged her too. Usually, he was just like Aliyah: not much of a hugger.

"I'm really proud of you, Aliyah," he said. He looked happier than she'd seen him in a long time.

Aliyah took a deep, shaky breath. She told herself to be brave. "Dad?" she said. "Can I ask you something?"

He looked surprised. "Sure."

Her throat felt sticky. "Was it my fault you and Mum were fighting all the time? It seemed you guys only started fighting after I started getting into trouble in school."

Her dad's face fell a little. "Oh, honey. No, of course not. Mum and I had our own problems. But we both love you very much." He hugged her again. "I'm so sorry if you've been thinking that. Thanks for asking me."

Aliyah's throat unstuck a little. "Thanks, Dad," she croaked. She could barely talk. It felt like the last bits of the knot in her belly had loosened.

Zoya came over and announced. "I want to stay in karate and work with Aliyah!"

"You've proved that you can work hard and be disciplined," said her dad. "We're very proud of you."

Suma hugged Aliyah, who was getting more hugs in one day than she'd had all year. "Thanks so much, Aliyah. You made such a difference. Seriously."

"No problem," said Aliyah, her throat still tight.

"Can we keep working together, Aliyah?" asked Zoya.

"Sure, if you want," said Aliyah.

"And," said Suma, "after Zoya accepts her medal, we're going to go out for ice cream. You and your dad are both invited. Do you want to come?"

Aliyah glanced at her dad. He nodded shyly. She realized he probably wasn't used to making new friends, either.

Aliyah took a deep breath and smiled at Suma. "Sure. We'll come."

Author Bio

Salima Alikhan has been a freelance writer and illustrator for fourteen years. She lives in Austin, Texas, USA, where she writes and illustrates children's books. Salima also teaches creative writing at St. Edward's University and English at Austin Community College. Her books and art can be found at www.salimaalikhan.net.

Glossary

aggression hostile or violent behaviour or attitude towards another person

back fist strike a punch thrown with the back of the fist

dojo gathering place for students of martial arts

dojo kun a term that means "training hall rules" in Japanese, and is used to mean the code or morals for certain dojos or types of karate

foot sweep a martial arts move used to trip an opponent

jab a quick, sharp blow or punch

reach the distance you can stretch your arm or leg to punch or kick something

roundhouse kick a kick made with a wide sweep of the leg and rotation of the body

sensei a martial arts teacher

side kick kick made with the kicking leg extending outwards, striking with the outside edge of the foot

spar to fight with an opponent in a short bout or practice session

tap out to tap the floor to show that you accept that your competitor has beaten you

MORE ABOUT
KARATE!

Aliyah, Zoya and Suma enjoy the sport of karate and all it has to offer. Would you be interested in learning more about karate?

For more information about karate and its history, check out some of these quick facts.

Karate was created on the island of Okinawa.

The full name of karate is "karate-do", which means "the way of the empty hand" in English.

There are many different styles of karate. The four major styles are called: Goju-ryu, Shotokan-ryu, Wado-ryu and Shito-ryu.

Because the Okinawans weren't allowed to use official weapons, they learned to use their farm tools as weapons! For example, nunchucks were once used to thresh rice and soybeans. The kama, which is similar to a crescent-shaped blade called a sickle, was used for reaping crops.

For the first time, karate will soon be featured in the Olympics! Participants will compete in kumite and kata. Kata means the forms, or movements, performed during karate. Kumite means active sparring with an opponent.

Discussion questions

1. According to Sensei Juarez, karate is about more than just competition. What are some of the other important things about karate? Do you think they're important? Why or why not?

2. Aliyah felt a strong connection to Zoya straight away. Why do you think that was?

3. When Aliyah heard her parents fighting, it was scary for her and made her angry. How did this make her act differently around other people? Can you think of a time that you were scared or angry, and it made you act differently towards people?

WRITING PROMPTS

1. Suma is Aliyah's rival, but do you think Suma feels the same way about Aliyah that Aliyah feels about her? Choose a scene and rewrite it from Suma's perspective. How would it be different?

2. Zoya doesn't like learning from Sensei Juarez, but she is willing to learn from Aliyah. Write about a time when it was easy for you to learn from a teacher, coach or sensei. Or write about a time when it was hard to learn from someone. What do teachers or coaches do that makes you want to learn or not learn?

3. Aliyah was worried that she was the reason her parents got in fights. If she had known it wasn't her fault all along, how do you think she would have behaved differently?

KEEP THE SPORTS ACTION GOING...

DISCOVER MORE SPORTS STORIES AT

www.raintree.co.uk